LOTS AND LOTS OF ZEBRA STRIPES

PATTERNS IN NATURE

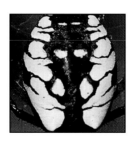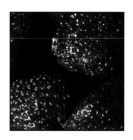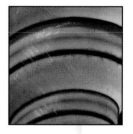

WRITTEN AND PHOTOGRAPHED BY

STEPHEN R. SWINBURNE

Boyds Mills Press

Foreword

Everywhere you go, you can find patterns in nature. They can be up in the clouds, or down in the sand. You might see a pattern in a cat's fur, a bird's feather, or a butterfly's wing. Some patterns are big like rainbows and some are small like a spider's web. You can even find a pattern in your favorite snack—a pineapple or watermelon. Once you begin to see the circles, stripes, and spirals in nature, you will find patterns in lots of places.

Many patterns have a purpose. The rings of a tree tell its age. The stripes on a garter snake act as a disguise. His pattern helps him hide. And many patterns are just beautiful to look at—the ripples on a pond, the frost on a window, or the piles of soap bubbles at bath time.

Certain patterns are unique. Did you know that no two snowflakes are alike? Did you know that no two zebras have the same pattern of stripes and no two giraffes have the same pattern of dark patches?

You may have seen some of the patterns in this book before, while some may be new. If you visit the zoo or go to a park, beach, or pond, it's fun to go on a pattern hunt. How many patterns can you find right outside your door?

—Steve Swinburne

Patterns are lines and shapes that repeat.

Some patterns are simple and some are not.

You can find patterns in

spring,

summer,

fall,

and winter.

Patterns can be circles or spots.

Patterns can be stripes or lines.

Patterns can be spirals.

Patterns can be found on the fur of animals

or the feathers of a bird.

Patterns can be found on the scales of a snake

or the shell of a turtle.

Some patterns show growth.

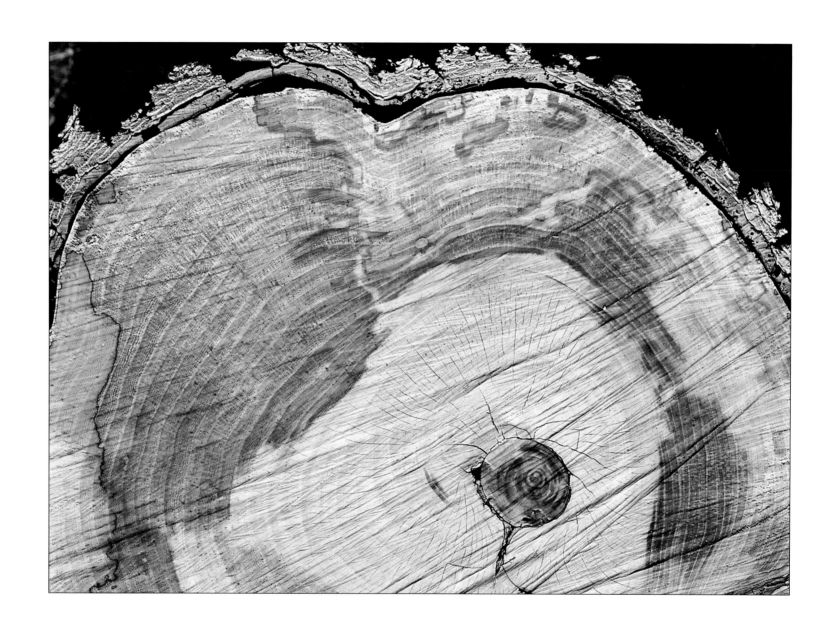

Some patterns show age.

Some patterns are straight lines.

Some patterns are curved lines.

Some patterns last only a short time.

Some patterns last forever.

You can find patterns in a park,

on a pond,

at a beach,

or on the forest floor.

Finding a pattern is fun.

Look for patterns where you live.

Can you find patterns in your lunch snack?

Can you find patterns on shells?

Can you find patterns in vegetables?

Can you find patterns on insects?

Can you find patterns on trees?

Can you find patterns on flowers?

Patterns make our world a beautiful place.

To the marvelous Spassoff boys,
Sebby and Sasha, and to Steffi and Bo,
without whom there would be no marvelous
Spassoff boys.

—S.S.

Many thanks to the children of Pamela Becker's kindergarten class at the
Brattleboro Central School, Brattleboro, Vermont, and the children of the
West River Montessori School, South Londonderry, Vermont. Thanks, too,
to Wendy Birkemeier, Linda Bailey, Barbara Kouts, Ellen Clyne,
and Advanced Imaging, Manchester, Vermont.

Text and photographs copyright © 1998 by Stephen Swinburne

Published by Caroline House • Boyds Mills Press, Inc. • A Highlights Company
815 Church Street • Honesdale, Pennsylvania 18431
Printed in Hong Kong

Publisher Cataloging-in-Publication Data
Swinburne, Stephen
Lots and lots of zebra stripes : patterns in nature / by
Stephen Swinburne.—1st.ed. • [32] p. : col. ill. ; cm.
Summary: A photo-essay featuring patterns that appear in
nature, from animal colorings to physical phenomena.
ISBN 1-56397-707-9
1. Nature photography—Juvenile literature. 2. Color of
animals—Juvenile literature. 3. Camouflage (Biology)—
Juvenile literature. [1. Nature photography. 2. Color of
animals. 3. Camouflage (Biology).] I. Title.
778.9—dc21   1998   AC   CIP
Library of Congress Catalog Card Number 97-77909

First edition, 1998
Book designed by Stephen Swinburne and Cathy Pernice
The text of this book is set in 24pt. Garamond

10 9 8 7 6 5 4 3 2 1